D0436008

SEAHORSE REEF
A Story of the South Pacific

SMITHSONIAN OCEANIC COLLECTION

For the children in Handumon village school—S.M.W.

To Dr. Amanda Vincent and the people at Project Seahorse for all they do to preserve one of nature's treasures—S.J.P.

Book copyright © 2000 Trudy Corporation and the Smithsonian Institution.

Published by Soundprints Division of Trudy Corporation, Norwalk, Connecticut.

All rights reserved. No part of this book may be reproduced or transmitted in any form or by any means whatsoever without prior written permission of the publisher.

Art Direction: Diane Hinze Kanzler; Ashley Andersen
Book layout: Shields & Partners, Westport, Connecticut; Scott Findlay
Editor: Judy Gitenstein

First Edition 2000
10 9 8 7 6 5 4 3 2
Printed in China

Acknowledgments:
  Our thanks to Tamsen M. Gray, museum specialist, Department of Invertebrates of the Smithsonian Instituion's National Zoological Park for her curatorial review.
  The author would like to thank Jonathan Anticamara, Dr. Amanda Vincent, and Dr. Elanor Bell of Project Seahorse for their advice and patience. Their study of seahorses educates us all.
  The illustrator would like to thank Peg Siebert at Blodget Memorial Library for extensive loan of research materials for this project; Diane Hinze Kanzler for guidance and research assistance, the researchers at Project Seahorse, the curators at the Smithsonian Institution, and his family for their support.

SEAHORSE REEF
A Story of the South Pacific

by Sally M. Walker   Illustrated by Steven James Petruccio

Soundprints
Where Children Discover...

The water surrounding the Danajon Bank, a double barrier reef in the Central Philippines, gets darker as the sun sinks toward the horizon. A seahorse's tail curls tightly around a branch of staghorn coral as its slender, upright body sways back and forth in the gentle current. Seahorse hides during the daytime. Even at night, when Seahorse moves around, he never goes very far. He always stays in the same small area. His mate roams a much larger area of the reef.

A Tiger cowrie extends its foot and glides across the bottom. A black backed butterfly fish swims by and nibbles on the tip of a coral branch. Then the butterfly fish slips under the edge of a piece of coral and settles for the night. The brown-and-yellow stripes on Seahorse's tail blend perfectly with his coral holdfast, making it hard for other fish to see him. He can see all around him, though. Now his right eye circles upward, while his left eye looks down. Because he has a neck, he can also bend his head up and down as he looks around.

Just then, Seahorse's mate swims out from behind a lettuce coral. As she gets closer, Seahorse lets go of his holdfast and swims toward her.

Seahorse passes a crown-of-thorns sea star and brushes by a sea whip. The abdomen of Seahorse's mate is swollen with eggs. The pouch on Seahorse's tail, up close to his belly, is flat and empty. Seahorse bends his body forward. The movement causes the top of his pouch to open. This movement means his pouch is ready for her eggs.

Seahorse and his mate point their tube-shaped snouts toward the water's surface and float upward together. The female's ovipositor—a special tube for laying eggs—deposits bright orange eggs into the male seahorse's pouch. In just a few seconds, the male's pouch becomes big and round.

Now that the eggs are safely in Seahorse's pouch and have been fertilized, they can begin to grow. Seahorse sinks back to the bottom and holds on to a coral. He rocks his body gently to settle the eggs inside his pouch. Seahorse's mate swims away. Only the male seahorse will care for and nourish the eggs inside his pouch.

Seahorse spends most of his time on the lookout for food. He eats tiny creatures that swim near his holdfast. A school of five-lined snapper swims nearby. They gobble up animals too big to fit inside Seahorse's tiny mouth and tube-shaped snout.

Seahorse uncurls his tail. The dorsal fin on his back flutters rapidly and pushes him upright through the water. The pectoral fin on each side of his head helps him steer around a sea anemone's stinging tentacles and the clown fish resting among them. The gill opening on each side of Seahorse's head opens and closes, pulling water into his body. Inside the opening, Seahorse's gills, shaped like a cluster of grapes, take the oxygen he needs from the water.

12

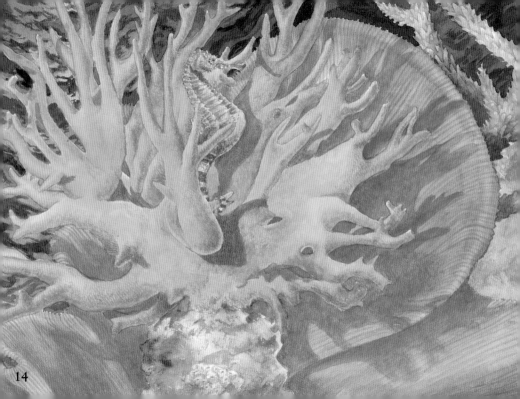

Seahorse senses a loud crunching sound. Danger is near! He tilts forward and stretches out his neck so he can swim quickly to a branching coral and hide. On the way, Seahorse brushes against the lettuce coral's rough edge. It scrapes Seahorse's skin. Seahorse has no scales. Skin stretches tightly over the knobby edges of the many bony plates that make up his skeleton. When Seahorse reaches the coral, his tail grabs hold and he stays perfectly still.

A parrotfish swims into view. The parrotfish is not a threat to Seahorse. He is busy biting off chunks of coral. His beak crunches the coral into bits so he can eat the plants and algae growing on it. Soon, the parrot fish will settle for the night. Slimy mucus is starting to cover his body. It will protect him while he sleeps.

Seahorse stays by the coral. Gradually the color of Seahorse's body changes and matches it perfectly. Seahorse's color camouflage hides him. If he stays for a long time, small bits of brown algae may catch on the ridges on top of his head. That will make it even harder for predators to spot him.

Nearby, a small hermit crab with a sea anemone on its shell rests on the top of a sea fan. Its pincers wave at a sea snake that swims by. The crab doesn't notice Seahorse. Finally, the crab climbs down the sea fan and scuttles away.

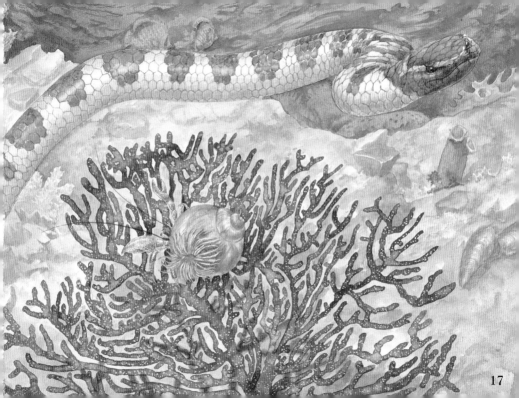

A Sergeant major swims across a flat area nearby. Suddenly, the bottom seems to explode. An octopus that has been hiding under a coral overhang rolls forward and startles the fish. The octopus rises up and jets backward through the water.

19

The octopus' movement has stirred up shrimp and the larvae of other fish. Seahorse's head darts forward. His lower lip, which folds up over the end of his snout, drops open. In an instant, Seahorse sucks in a shrimp and his lower lip flips back up. Seahorse has no teeth, so he swallows the shrimp whole. He sucks in larvae and shrimp until the water current carries them out of his reach.

Seahorse's eyes look in all directions as he watches and waits for more prey. To stay healthy he must eat a few thousand of the tiny creatures each day.

Seahorse's babies have been growing inside his pouch for about three weeks. During that time Seahorse has been busy eating a lot of food. That has helped the fluid in his pouch keep the babies clean and healthy. As the babies have grown, the pouch fluid has become salty, like the ocean water. The babies wiggle inside fleshy pockets inside Seahorse's pouch. They are ready to be born.

Seahorse relaxes the muscle at the top of his pouch until the hole at the top of the pouch opens. Seahorse bends his tail forward and upward. His movement squeezes a burst of baby seahorses from his pouch, then another and another until his pouch is empty.

Seahorse gives birth to more than three hundred baby seahorses. Their eyes and snouts look huge compared to the rest of their bodies. Even though they are very tiny, the babies know how to swim. The babies will be on their own, for Seahorse and his mate do not take care of their babies at all.

Some of the babies sink to the bottom. Their tails quickly grab the nearest holdfast. Other babies have curled their tails around each other. In a group they drift about in the water. All of the babies start looking for food as soon as possible. If they don't find food, they will starve.

Normally, only one or two babies from each brood will grow to adulthood. Most of the babies are eaten by fish or they starve when water currents sweep them away.

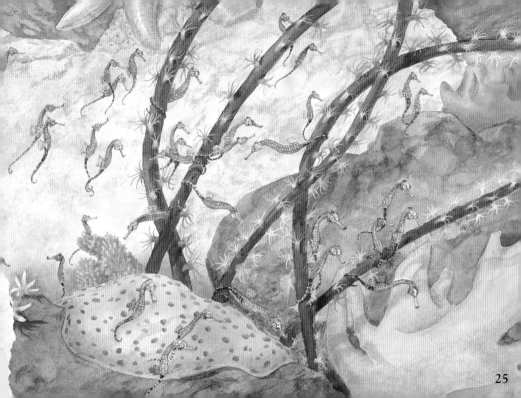

Seahorse rests after the babies are born. It is nighttime on the reef. Some animals are sleeping, but many are awake. A nurse shark cruises past the lettuce coral where Seahorse is resting.

A moray eel has just finished its dinner. It wriggles halfway out of the hole where it lives and opens its mouth. Sharp white teeth gleam in the dim light. Soon a little fish swims into the eel's mouth. But the eel doesn't eat the fish. The fish is a cleaner wrasse. Every night the cleaner wrasse eats parasites — harmful creatures — from inside the eel's mouth. This keeps the eel healthy.

Suddenly, Seahorse feels a sharp pinch. Something is pulling him.

A swimmer crab has grabbed Seahorse's tail. The crab pulls Seahorse away from the coral. Seahorse twists and turns his body. He pulls free and wedges his body tightly inside the lettuce coral. The crab pushes its pincer into the crack. The claws open and close. They nip at Seahorse's tail again and again, but can't grab hold. The deep ridges of the lettuce coral help protect Seahorse.

Finally the crab gives up. Seahorse is safe. His tail is cut, but it will heal. Seahorse hides in the coral for the rest of the night.

As the sun rises, the water surrounding the Danajon Bank looks blue-green. Seahorse peeks out from the lettuce coral. He sees his mate. Her abdomen is swollen with new eggs. Seahorse's pouch is empty. He is ready to care for new eggs. Seahorse leaves the coral and swims toward his mate.

About the Seahorse

There are thirty-two different species of seahorse. They range in size from the tiny half-inch-long Hippocampus barbiganti to the fourteen-inch Hippocampus abdominalis. Seahorses live in salt water from 3 to 80 feet deep in places where water temperatures range from 43°F to 86°F. In addition to coral reefs, seahorses inhabit mangrove swamps, estuaries, and sea grass beds.

Some species of seahorse hold "daily greetings." Each day the female seahorse visits her mate for several minutes. Their color turns bright and they swim together with entwined tails. Biologists think the daily greeting reinforces the pair bond between seahorse mates. Other species, like Hippocampus comes, do not hold daily greetings.

Female seahorse's bodies bulge when the eggs are ready to be transferred. In contrast, a male's pouch is flat when he is able to receive them. Seahorse eggs are fertilized in the male's pouch.

Seahorses are not strong swimmers. However, their upright posture is perfect for slipping between coral branches, mangrove roots, and blades of sea grass. The tiny pectoral fins allow seahorses to turn easily. Seahorses can even swim in an upward spiral. One wave of a seahorse's dorsal fin is faster than the human eye can see.

Each year more than twenty million seahorses are removed from the oceans for use in traditional medicines, home aquariums, and as curios, such as key chains. Coastal development and the mining of reefs for cement production destroy seahorse habitats. To help seahorses, some villages in the southwest Pacific are establishing sanctuaries. These protected areas give seahorses, other fish, and the habitats a chance to rebound and recover.

Glossary

brood: The group of babies that is growing inside a seahorse's pouch.

dorsal fin: The fin on a seahorse's back.

holdfast: Any object a seahorse wraps its tail around to keep it in place.

larva: A young stage of a fish's development.

prehensile: Able to grab and hold objects.

prey: An animal that is hunted as food.